One Snowy Night

M. Christina Butler

Tina Macnaughton

LITTLE TIGER PRESS

The cold wind woke Little Hedgehog from his deep winter sleep. It blew his blanket of leaves high into the air, and he shivered in the snow.

Suddenly, something fell from the sky . . . .

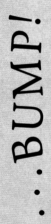

...BUMP!

It was a package, and it had his name on it.

To Little Hedgehog
With Love From
Father Christmas xx

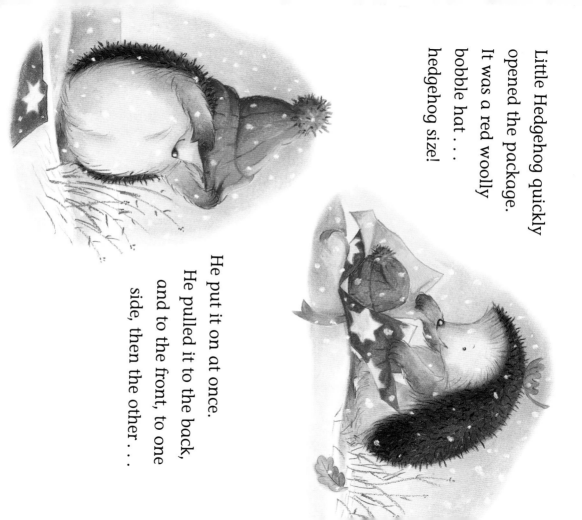

Little Hedgehog quickly
opened the package.
It was a red woolly
bobble hat . . .
hedgehog size!

He put it on at once.
He pulled it to the back,
and to the front, to one
side, then the other . . .

But his prickles got in the way every time.
Now the hat was far too big for
a little hedgehog.

So he wrapped it up again,
tore a bit off the label,
and wrote on the rest.

Happy Christmas Rabbit
with love from
Little Hedgehog xx

Then off he ran to Rabbit's house.
Rabbit was out, so he left the present
on his doorstep.

It was snowing hard as Little Hedgehog
tried to find his way back home.

"Oh dear, oh dear," he said. "I shouldn't
have come out in this weather. But I'm
sure Rabbit will be pleased to have
a nice woolly hat."

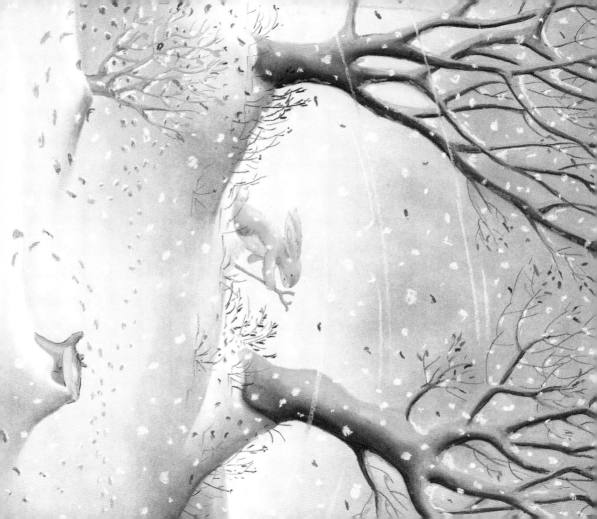

"What's this?" Rabbit squeaked with delight, ripping off the paper. "A bobble hat," he cried. "For ME!"

He tried it with his ears inside, and then outside. He pulled it this way and that way. But his ears got in the way . . . *every time!*

By now the hat was far too big for a rabbit. So he took it to Badger.

"What . . . about . . . THAT!" said Badger.

"Very nice," said Rabbit.

"What did you say?" asked Badger.

"*Very nice!*" yelled Rabbit,
hopping off.

So he wrapped up the
package and marched
off to Fox's house.

"Don't you like it?" asked
Badger. But Rabbit had left.
"This is no good to me,"
he said. "I can't hear
a thing."

Fox was going out exploring.
"What's this?" he asked grumpily.
"A Christmas present, especially for you!"
said Badger kindly. "Merry Christmas!"
And he plodded off.

He made two holes for
his ears and put it on.
Pleased, he went on
his way.

"A hat?" sneered Fox.
"What do I want with
a hat?"
Then he looked at
the hat again . . .

The white fields twinkled in the
moonlight. Fox sniffed around and
found a small trail. He followed it this way
and that way until suddenly it stopped.
There was something under the snow!

Fox dug and dug, until he
found a hedgehog. It was
cold and did not move.
"Poor little fellow," he said.
He put the hedgehog
inside the red woolly hat
and carried it to
Rabbit's house.

Rabbit and Badger were having supper.

"Look what I've found in the snow!"
cried Fox, bursting in.

"It's Little Hedgehog!" cried Rabbit.
"He must have gotten lost going home!"

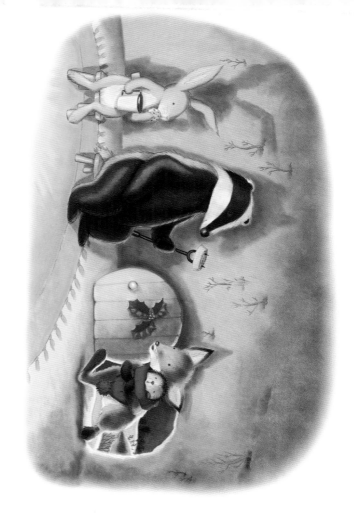

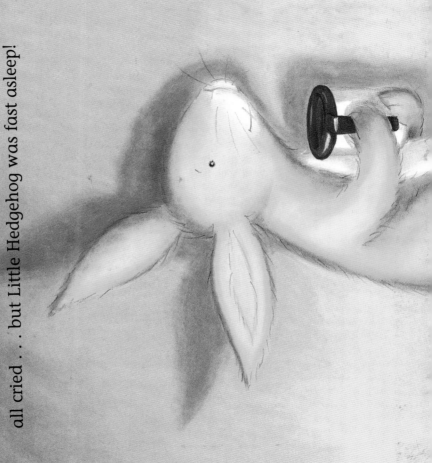

"Hello," said Little Hedgehog sleepily.

"Oh, this is such a lovely warm blanket."

"I think this woolly hat is *just right*
for you!" said Badger.

"Merry Christmas, Little Hedgehog!" they
all cried . . . but Little Hedgehog was fast asleep!